# 01
## UNPRETTY
"... YOU ARE MADE IN HIS IMAGE."

# 02
## REAL MEN
"REAL MEN ACT AS A BUILDING BLOCK."

# 03
## KEEP YOUR HEAD UP
"THIS ONE IS FOR THE MOTHERS..."

# 04
## BEAUTIFUL BLACK WOMEN
"YOU ARE MY STRENGTH."

---

TH*E* SOURCES OF MY STRE\NTH

## 05
## WHERE HAS THE LOVE GONE
"OUR GENERATION NOW PRAISES THINGS WHICH WILL PASS AWAY..."

## 06
## MUMMY
"WE'RE GOING TO MAKE YOU PROUD."

## 07
## HIS NAME IS JESUS
"I SHALL FEAR NO EVIL."

## 08
## NOT JUST A HOBBY
"IT'S A PLATFORM TO USE YOUR WORDS."

---

THE SOURCES OF MY STRENGTH

## 09
## I LOVE YOU
"I DON'T SAY IT OUT OF HABIT.."

## 10
## DADDY ARE YOU PROUD OF ME
"... FATHER BRING ME A NEW CIRCLE."

## 11
## AN UNFINISHED LETTER TO MY WIFE
"... WE'RE IN THIS TOGETHER, FOREVER."

## 13
## THERE'S ONLY ONE MJ
"BOYS SEEM TO THINK THEY'RE SMOOTH CRIMINALS..."

THE SOURCES OF MY STRENGTH

## 14
## GOD BLESS AMERICA
"REPAIR IT PLEASE!"

## 15
## WHEN YOU BELIEVE IN THAT GOD
"YOU CAN NEVER FAIL."

## 16
## FROM ME TO YOU
"... FEMALE VINCENT VAN GOGH."

## 17
## MELANIN MONROE
"...EVERY IMAGE OF A BLACK GIRL IS LIKE ART..."

THE SOURCES OF MY STRENGTH

# UNPRETTY

Dear ugly,
You aren't beautiful enough
You will never be as beautiful as the girls in the magazine
Oh my goodness
They never looked so clean
But in case you didn't know
The girls in the magazine
Don't even look like the girls in the magazine

But girls never seem to realise that
They never looked so good
Because his grace is your makeup
So keep your chin up
Cause all your imperfections add up
To create the Princess that reads this

We need to rise above the words
And keep God at the centre
You are queens and you don't need men to define you
Because the almighty God has worked his magic
And used his brush strokes to such perfection
That you are made in his image
There's a beauty in the roughness of your edges
There's elegance in the way your skin stretches
The greatest curve on a woman's body is her smile
And the way she carries herself with style

The times have changed
So now I say:

Dear Beautiful,
Stand up and stand out
Rise up and speak out
Because unpretty girls are now loved
Unpretty girls are now powerful
Unpretty girls are now strong
Unpretty girls are now winning
Unpretty girls are now unstoppable
Unpretty girls are now fierce
Unpretty girls are now fearless
Unpretty girls are now pretty

# REAL MEN

What defines a Real Man?
Is it whether they treat their women like queens
Or whether they are always on the scene

There's a difference between the title 'Dad' and 'Father'
Anybody can be a dad, but not everybody matures into a father
If you haven't got the heart for it don't bother

The world has real men
They always prove it time and again
Real men leave it to God
And let everything fall into place

Real men are showered with grace
As they run their race
And will never be a victim to disgrace

It's the actions not the words that make a real man
Because real men don't talk the talk but walk the walk
Real men act as a building block
And leave an in-heritage for their sons and daughters

Real men don't crumble under the words of the world
Or conform to the patterns of it
But grab the enemy by the neck
And shout, lord please take control
And let your spirit rest on my soul

Real men protect their own
And treat their family as if
The were sitting on the throne
Real men make stuff happen
Whether they shed blood, sweat or tears
They will never let their fears control them

# KEEP YOUR HEAD UP

This Is One For The Mothers, so just tune in....

The darkest hour is just before the dawn
Trust me the lord won't allow your children to mourn
It feels like your body is worn, torn
This is just a reminder it's about your turn, so...
Never let up, always live but don't forget
Mama keep your head up

You must feel like the enemy is pulling you into the pit
I know that even if you don't feel like it
Gods got you
He knows the beginning from the end
He's going to mend, defend, lend a helping hand
To heal you as planned
Then it's going to be like your living in dreamland

Philippians 4:13
I can do all things through Christ who strengthens me
Your body is about to be set free
From the physical bond of the enemy
You just need to remember that
God will never leave nor forsake you
Cause he's got a plan for you
After all is said and done
If Satan wants round two, just show him the bottom of your show

Never let up, always live but don't forget
Mama keep your head up

Real men make a way and leave a foot path so others can follow through
Real men don't leave their children wondering who their father is
And whether daddy is coming home for Christmas
Or worst of all if daddy has children elsewhere
But instead lift up the names of their children in prayer

Real men allow every mouth to get fed
And try their hardest to get everybody sleeping on a bed
Real men stand as one
Real men fear none
And give all the glory to the soon coming son

These are just some of the things that make up the real men in the world
There's a real man for every real female out there, keep your head up

# BEAUTIFUL BLACK WOMEN

Beautiful black women
You are my strength
Because I'd live and I'd die for you
Despite the fact many in this world look down on black men
Even taking the law into their own hands, bending and misusing it
You are still my source of strength

Yet ironically, Beautiful black women
You are my weakness also
Because you possess the keys to unlock doors on the inside of me
That society insists should be remained shut

The World builds a fire and anger on the inside of me
That can only be quenched by the softness of your words
And the gentleness of your touch

Beautiful black women is there anything you can not do
To tell you the truth
It baffles me how society can call you ugly and dirty
Cause from the moment I saw your face
I understood I had to protect you at all costs
Cause you are the queens of my race

Never hide your marks and your scars
Because they make up the very core of you
The true beauty of a black women is shown to us when,
When she constantly goes through trouble
And comes out better than when she entered

Never feel ashamed about your body or embarrassed by it
Instead I'd rather embrace it
What the world calls flaws
I call fabulous
What the world calls monstrosities
By God, I call it a masterpiece

Black Kings, we must
We must protect and love our kingdoms greatest treasure
Because nobody else will
Black kings love our black queens and show our princess' and princes
How they should be loved

Beautiful black women
The honest truth is
People disrespect what they don't understand
That's why they don't know where they stand
But beautiful black women never forget your value,
And don't let others forget it either
There are very few things more mesmerising
Than when the sun kisses the skin of a black women
And produces a sight to behold
With a skin tone that has a mix of chocolate and gold

The beautiful black women
Has been hunted down since time began
But it's now that we are beginning to realise
That they are the epitome of strength and courage

Beautiful black women
I will love you till the end of time
You are my place of comfort
You are my angel in a human disguise
Beautiful black women
You are so amazing, when I reach heaven I will paint pictures of you in the sky

You have immaculate natural skin
No diamond in the world compares to you
My beautiful black gem
So beautiful black women
Never forget you are a
Beautiful. Black. Women

# WHERE HAS THE LOVE GONE

Where has the love for our God gone
Our generation now praises things which will pass away
Unlike the word, which will always remain the same
We've lost so much respect for our God
That we now spell his name with a lower case 'G'
It's like… where has the love gone?

It's weird but sometimes I feel sorry for God
Cause he loves us unconditionally
But it's only when he puts money in our pocket,
Keys to a new car and clothes on our back that we begin loving him
Conditional love, the kind of love that doesn't get you too far

The kind of love that says
As long as your bum is big I may not love you,
but I'll love it just to make you smile
As long as you stimulate sexually,
I'll love the feeling for the time being
It's that unconditional love that loves you through the cold and the rain
That love that warms your insides,
Even when your going through different storms
It's that unconditional love that God provides

We take for granted a God that…
A God that stands for us every morning, day and night
This so called thing we live in – the flesh
Our temporary home, has lost sight of the end goal
Spending eternity in heaven with our father
The same father we don't even think to thank at anytime
It's got to the stage where
Where we can't even differentiate whether it's God
Or if we have some sort of power of our own

The craziest thing of all is that
We serve a God who still loves us unconditionally
Despite the fact we forsake him more than we cherish him
So I ask you the question:
Where has your love gone?

# MUMMY

Mummy I'm going to love you till the day I die
It broke my heart the first time I ever saw you cry
You gave birth to three
We're like the three musketeers
We're going to make you proud
So you don't ever find tears

I love the way you keep your head up,
You don't let, even though others around you gave up
Trust me, I can't wait
Till the point where you put your feet up and rest
So that I put my money to the test… for you

For you I will do anything
Because you gave me everything
I know you're going to love the female who wears my engagement ring
You raised me to make an impact like M.L King
My mummy, my queen - you're apart of my foundation
I can't wait to get to the top, so you can see your baby boy shining
Mummy I'm coming, just wait on me
But until then never forget…

Mummy I love you

# HIS NAME IS JESUS

His Name is Jesus
The faithful God of yesterday and Today
I feel his presence whenever I pray
Whenever my sky looks grey
I just look up and say
Jesus please guide my day

He gives me a burning desire
To make me go higher
And prove the devil is a liar
But don't let it be me they admire
Just know you as the only messiah

Jesus allows me to know that
I shall fear no evil
And I shall trample over serpents and snakes
And not even worry about the fakes
But remember that my king is triumphant
And the man who makes the enemy redundant

The devil wants to take my glory
He tried to make me naked
He tried and tried
He caught me with my head down and got excited
Until I looked up to the most high and said amen
…Until I looked up to the most high and said amen

# POETRY, IT'S NOT JUST A HOBBY

Poetry it's not just a hobby
It's a platform to use your words how you please
It's gives you an opportunity to explain your love for the one who lives above the sky
Or exclaim your hate for the one who is not so high

Poetry, it gives you a sense of freedom
At times it has you feeling on top of the world
But other times it has you feeling like the world is on top of you
Cause it just becomes one of those nights
Where you feel like taking the long way home
Cause all your problems and issues rise to the surface
And you have no other choice but to write

But poetry, it hasn't been as kind to me recently
To tell you the truth it's kind of been doing me dirty
But I still say thank you,
You've put me on different stages
And you've made my words melt in the hearts of the people

So I bid you a farewell, just for now
Until I get my MoJo back somehow
You won't be seeing me around
I'm sitting here at 3:30am
Thinking how much you've done for me
Put me at ease
Don't see this as a cancellation
But just a temporary freeze

Cause poetry, it's not just a hobby
You kept me standing when I was groggy
You kept me firm when I was rocky
So thank you...
Cause you weren't just a hobby

# I LOVE YOU

When I say 'I love you'
I don't say it out of habit
I say it to remind you that
You are the best thing to ever happen to me

I know you fear the future
You are scared of whether I'm going to change
Or whether I'm going to be just like your father
Or even if I'm going to find another girl who'll make my smile larger
I assure you that's not going to happen

You made me realise that
What's 100 favourites
when your favourite can't get through to you
Cause you're busy with the other 99

You make me so happy
You got me feeling like Shakespeare
Saying stuff like
Shall I compare thee to a summers day
You even got me saying stuff like
I hate all the letters in the alphabet
But I love you

See I'm a boring young brother
No drama, no stories, no history
I always laugh when you call me a mystery
Cause I don't say what's on my mind

A long time ago
I realised I was thinking of you
And I began to wonder how long you'd been on my mind
Then it dawned on me
Since I met you
You never left

See you've left your mark
See you've been there from the start
And I can't wait to finish this with you

You got me writing unfinished letters to my wife
Cause you are my Melanin Monroe
Im only telling you the truth
Because you are the girl of my dreams
But I keep asking myself the question
Can I get it right?

Time and time again
I find myself flicking through...
Flicking through old photos and videos of you
And just thinking to myself
That your Imperfections to me
Are made perfect

As if you was hand picked
Hand picked by God
To be the girl who makes me a better man
You got me so in love
I'd be happy just being your doorman

I wish I could have this moment for life
Trust me, One day
I'm going to make you my wife
I wouldn't have it any other way

Everything starts off with a little bit of friendship
But for me that ship sailed
Cause I got lost in your dark brown eyes
The depth of your mind
Has me looking up to the sky
Wondering when will my dreams
of being with you come true

I said
The depth of your mind
Has me looking up to the sky
Wondering when will my dreams
of being with you come true

You tell me stories about how you used to like this guy
But he didn't like you back
But that brought me to the realisation
That one mans trash is another mans treasure

In my head I'm laughing
When you tell me the same guy that didn't like you two years back
Is now hitting up your phone
Trying to pick up his slack And get you back
Like settle down bro
There's a new leader of the pack

You're so good to me
I could find myself getting lost in you
I can't wait to go down on one knee
And just make it you and me

In case you didn't know
When I say 'I love you'
I don't say it out of habit
I say it to remind you that
You are the best thing to ever happen to me
I love you

# DADDY ARE YOU PROUD OF ME?

Daddy are you proud of me?
I know I may fall short of your glory
But daddy are you proud of me?
Have I done enough to get to heaven
I'm trying so hard to live my life like the number 7

Daddy don't allow your voice to fall on deaf ears
The bible says iron sharpens iron
I must be the sharpest amongst my pears
And if I'm not
Father bring me a new circle

Daddy are you proud of me?
I may not know what my purpose is now
But when I find it
I will attack it head on
Like a lion who is always up for a fight
I'm always looking to reach a new height

Daddy I want you to be so proud of me
That mere men on earth will see
The wonders you always do for me
I want to cry tears of joy for your name
I just want others to do the same
Trust me your name will never know shame

Daddy are you proud of me?

# AN UNFINISHED LETTER TO MY WIFE

This is a letter to my wife to be,
see I don't know where you are or what your doing
but I hope your doing something meaningful
The future apple of my eye
The perfect woman for me
I don't know what your going through right now
But I know my Gods going to sort it out

I don't know if your like other girls
Who seem to think Everyman they fall for
Is going to fall in love with another girl
But the sad truth is that I am
And she is going to call you mummy

I don't care what mistakes you have made
Or what mistakes your going to make
Cause we're in this together, forever
I don't believe in no divorce or annulments
See when we have an argument
I'm going to give you your space
Then I'm going to bring you back and sort it out for two reasons
First because I love and appreciate you
And second
Because our children are only going to see us smiling

I'm going to treat you like the queen you are
Not just because your a shining star
But anything else would just be below par
You see where going to be a family of royalty
Not purely because we are fulfilling purpose
But simply because we look amazing

This is an unfinished letter because I can't tell the future
Nor can I live it without you
This story is what we are going to finish together
Just wait and see

This is my unfinished letter to my wife to be

# THERE IS ONLY ONE MJ

Boys seem to think they're smooth criminals
But really they need to take a look at the man in the mirror
And bring God nearer
We need to stop falling for these Dirty Diana's
Or these Pretty Young Things
But Instead act like kings
Boys we need to learn how to beat it when we get the wrong feeling
Cause going sexual isn't the only healing

Girls need to find God
Cause his love never felt so good
Instead of trying to be billie jeans
You should be trying to get to the top by all means
It doesn't matter if your black or white
Because you are not alone
It's time for you queens to step up to the throne
Your beauty needs to be shown
It's human nature to not trust God
But he's telling you I'll be there when you need me
Just wait and see that all jehovah wants to do is
hold your hand and make your name grand

Nobody seems to remember the time
When God had them
Even though they did the crime
And we're able to sleep peacefully come bedtime
It's as simple as ABC, one two three
You don't have to pay an admissions fee
You just need to know God holds the key
Which will allow you to live joyfully

# GOD BLESS AMERICA

You're mouths shout 'We come to protect and serve'
But your actions speak otherwise
Black lives scared about if they'll even make it to sunrise
Cause nowadays it's like killing someone of colour is the ultimate prize

When I say to God RIP
I don't mean Rest In Peace
I mean Repair It Please
So that they can Remain In peace

Who do we call when we're in trouble
Cause it's police who are breaking the laws
Maybe we should called them outlaws
Here to 'Steal and Smile'
Cause they didn't even get put on trial

Let's not get ahead of ourselves
Let's not forget the officers who follow the motto
'Protect and Serve'
They should get the credit they deserve

God Bless America
Too many kings and queens dying
Leaving family members crying
If only you knew
It's just so terrifying

Black men are scared to raise their hands
Cause they'll end with 6 warning shots in their back
And everything just goes pitch black

God Bless America
Cause when I say RIP
I don't mean Rest In Peace
I mean Repair it Please

So they can Remain In Peace

# WHEN YOU BELIEVE IN THAT GOD

See you need to find something to believe in
Cause when you believe in my God
You can never fail
With my God it's not a matter of being male or female
Funny how with my God it's not a matter of you live and you learn
But my God changes it to you win and you earn

When you believe in that God
He does wonders
That God that will never let his children be put asunder
My God commands thunder
And never even makes a blunder
But turned a boy who was once under to the boy wonder

In case you didn't catch it I was talking about myself
From a boy who didn't love himself
Who wanted so desperately to find himself
So that one day his name will be placed on the top shelf

A boy who had a terrible stutter
And was scared to utter..
Utter a word
Cause he thought people laughed every time he spoke
He though he was the primary school joke

Until the one funny day he opened this pretty thick book called the bible
And realised he held quite a strong title
And that was winner
See that boy was a winner of his battles
And he shook off every single shackle
And had the strength to tackle...
Tackle his challenges head on

When you believe in that God
You can do anything
Because he's given you the power to do everything
My God has made me to believe that even though I walk through the valley
of the shadow of death I shall fear no evil because they rod and thy staff
comfort me
I have complete trust in he
Because he has made me see
That when you believe in the almighty God
The impossible is made possible

When you believe in that God
He turns a boy into a man
And fills him with a plan
To take a stand
And become the man he was set out to become
When you believe in that God
That's what he does for you

# FROM ME TO YOU

I never get tired of writing about my love for you
I'll keep writing about how I love you
Even up until the point my face turns blue
I'm going to try and make you understand this
You're like the female Vincent Van Gogh
You were the artist and my heart was the canvas

Each brush stroke was so precious
They made a man out of this mess
See the way you loved me at times had me breathless

It was the amount skill you had in your fingers
As if you were painting an image matched only by the Mona Lisa
So I'd release her to carry on as her fingers tell me a story
A story with no words but just the slow caressing and transfer of heat
That let me know she loves me and wants me to stay

You turned a stary night into some blossoming chestnut branches
You made the days feel warm again, you had me feeling for you..
you had me feeling for you like a man gone off cocaine

So this letter is from me to you
This is just a sneak preview
I wrote this to help pull me through..
pull me through the nights you aren't here
Just so your artwork don't disappear
Just so your artwork don't disappear

# MELANIN MONROE

See me I need a Melanin Monroe
If you don't get it let me explain it to you
See a Melanin Monroe is a beautiful black queen
Who is going to step up in the scene
And take it by storm

See me I need a Melanin Monroe
A girl who is never going to hear the word no
Cause she is going to open doors for herself
And her name is always going to be on the top shelf
She is going to tower above the rest
And she is always going to be amongst the best

See me I need a melanin Monroe
A girl that takes my breath away
Every time I think of her
Cause every image of a black girl is like art
Her eyes always tell me a story
And her smile captures the very essence of who she is
And I love that

See me I need a Melanin Monroe
You just need to unleash your beauty
Because beauty flows from the heart
Trust me, this is just the start
The start of something amazing
An uprising of queens
Because behind every great man
Is an even greater women

See me I need a Melanin Monroe
My Monroe is going to be my big cuddly teddy bear
Whom I can't help but stare
Asking myself, why are you so rare
See me I need a Melanin Monroe

Blank Page

Blank Page

# About the Poet

Joseph Omole is a talented and poetic young man. At just 18, he compiled his first volume of poems. He is an excellent leader to many and an inspiration to all. When it comes to writing, he likes to write about current political and social issues surrounding young people, the black community and faith. When Joseph gets older he hopes to impact his community through his poetry and positive social action projects.

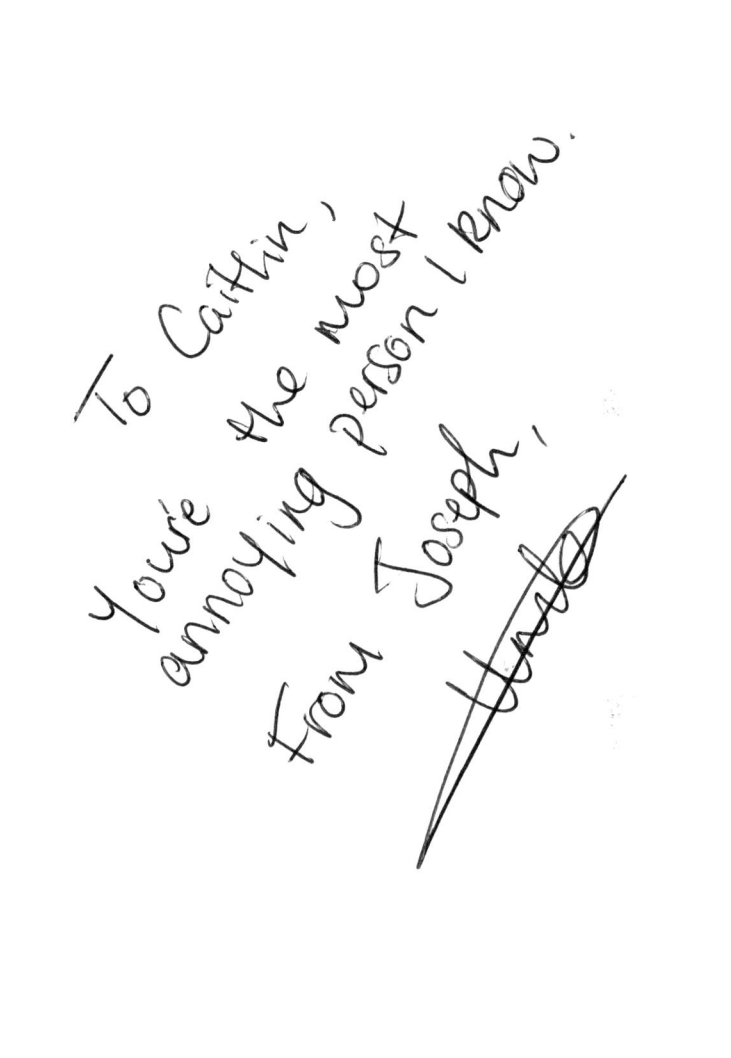
To Caitlin,
You're the most annoying person I know.
From Joseph,

Printed in Great Britain
by Amazon